Disney Bunnies

my first Bedtime storybook

Disney PRESS

Los Angeles • New York

Published by Disney Press, an imprint of Disney Book Group. No part of this book may
be reproduced or transmitted in any form or by any means, electronic or mechanical,
including photocopying, recording, or by any information storage and retrieval
system, without written permission from the publisher. For information address
Disney Press, 1200 Grand Central Avenue, Glendale, California 91201.

First Hardcover Edition, January 2020 10 9 8 7 6 5 4 3 2 1
ISBN 978-1-368-05269-6

FAC-025393-19284

Library of Congress Control Number: 2019936650
Printed in China

For more Disney Press fun, visit www.disneybooks.com

Contents

This book belongs to:

_____

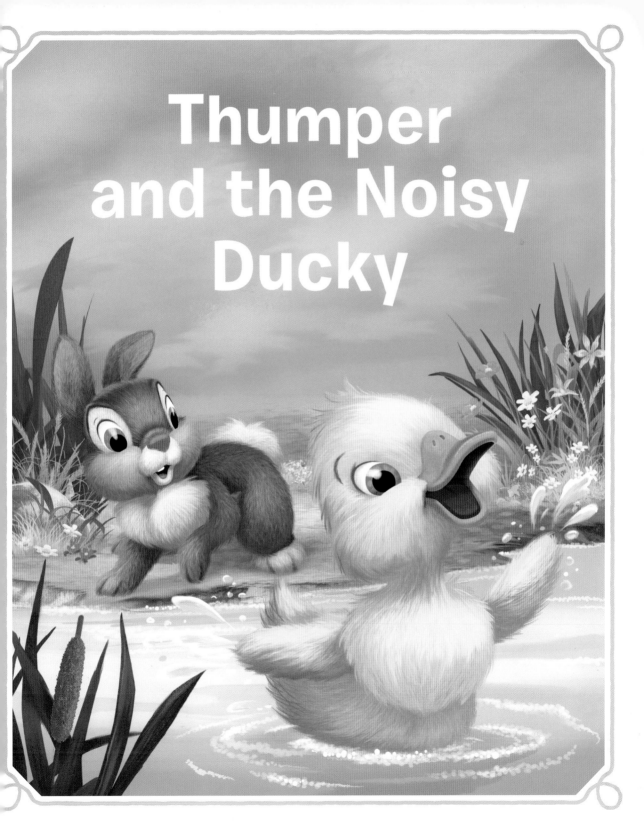

Thumper and the Noisy Ducky

One warm spring afternoon, the bunnies were all nestled in the SOFT CLOVER for a nap.

Thumper was having a sweet dream when suddenly he was awoken by a sound. . . .

"QUACK!"

Thumper followed the sound and found a noisy little duckling.

"QUACK! QUACK!" said the ducky.

"Shhh," said Thumper.

Thumper pointed at his sisters, who were still fast asleep.

"Quack," he whispered softly.

"QUACK!" the ducky trumpeted.

Thumper sighed and then settled down to nap once more. "Shhh," he said sleepily.

But the little ducky didn't understand. He hopped onto Thumper's back. "QUACK?"

Soon the duckling's sisters waddled over and gathered around Thumper.

"QUACK? QUACK?" all the little duckies said.

Suddenly, Thumper had an idea. "QUACK!" he said loudly.

The ducklings jumped and flapped their little wings. Thumper's sisters woke up. When they saw the ducklings, they jumped, too. Then the bunnies and the duckies all GIGGLED and QUACKED and giggle-quacked.

The ducklings and the bunnies had such fun playing together.

But after a while, the little ducky said, "SHHH!"

And the duckies and the bunnies settled down
into the soft clover for a quiet nap together.
SHHHHHH . . .

A Day with Papa

Thumper was EXCITED. He and his dad were
spending the day together. Thumper wondered what
Papa Bunny had planned. Maybe they would climb a
mountain . . . or explore a cave!

"I thought we'd gather some GREENS for supper," Papa Bunny said.

"Yes, Papa," said Thumper, his heart sinking.

Before too long, Thumper wanted a cool drink.

"Don't dawdle," said Papa Bunny.

"I won't, Papa," replied Thumper. And off he went.

While Thumper had some water, he saw ducks splashing. He WISHED he could join them.

But Thumper knew that Papa was waiting.

Thumper hadn't hopped very far before he saw his friend the opossum.

"Want to CLIMB THIS TREE with me?" the opossum asked.

"Okay!" Thumper said, forgetting about his papa. And with a little boost from his friend, Thumper was soon exploring the old oak tree.

The two friends woke up a sleepy owl.
"WHOO! WHOO!"

They said hello to some
baby birdies in a nest.
"CHIRP! CHIRP!"

They got close—but not
too close—to a buzzing
beehive. BUZZ! BUZZ!

"Well, it's time for me to go," the opossum said after a while. "My father is waiting for me."

UH-OH! Thumper remembered his own papa. Thumper looked down. The ground was very far away. How would he ever get down?

Thumper waited and waited. Then he waited some more. "Only one person can help me," he said.

"WHOOO?" asked the owl.

"My papa," said Thumper sadly.

"I thought you'd never ask!" said someone from below.

"PAPA?" Thumper asked hopefully.

"Yes, Thumper, it's me," Papa Bunny replied. "Now take a deep breath and look down."

Thumper opened his eyes to find his papa reaching for him.

Thumper reached down, and his father pulled him close. "You must never be afraid to ask me for help. I am your FATHER, and I will always be here for you," Papa Bunny said.

"I know, Papa," said Thumper.

"Well, all work and no play makes for a bored little
bunny!" said Papa Bunny. "Why don't we EXPLORE
a hidden cave? Then we'll race back to the meadow.
The last one there is a slowpoke!"

Thumper's Summer Day

One summer morning, the sun had just begun to come up. The CREATURES of the forest were beginning to stir.

But THUMPER and his sisters were already
wide-awake and ready to play.

As the sun rose higher and higher in the sky, it got warmer and warmer. So the bunnies decided to cool off in the stream.

SPLISH, SPLASH!

Then they HOPPED to a hidden hollow. Inside the hollow, it was cool and dark.

Later, as the sun crept across the sky, Thumper sailed across the pond. He waved HELLO to his beaver friend as he floated by.

The hot summer sun blazed on. The bunnies cloud-gazed as the fluffy shapes moved across the sky.

The bunnies berry-grazed until their **TUMMIES** were full.

Finally, the sun took a nap. The bunnies hopped
and danced as RAIN fell down.

As the sun began to set and the cool breeze of evening began to blow, the BUNNIES had a picnic.

The MOON came out. The sky grew darker.

The sun headed home, and so did the bunnies.

I Love You,
My Bunnies

Spring had finally arrived in the forest. Butterflies flitted from flower to flower. And robins sang cheerfully in the trees. "TWITTER, TWEET."

The bunnies' day began just the same as always—with a soft,

cozy nuzzle,

a filling of bunny
tummies,

and a big,
strong HUG.

Soon the bunnies hopped off to play.

"Mama does so much for us," Thumper said. "Let's make her a basket."

Thumper and his sisters HOPPED to it, searching high and low for twigs.

SCRITCH, SCRATCH. The bunnies wove the twigs together. They made a basket as strong as their love for their mama.

The basket was sturdy. But it needed something more. "Flowers!" Daisy cried.

SNIFF, SNIFF . . . PLUCK!

The bunnies picked buttercups and daisies and lilies. Little Tessie even found some pink clover.

They filled the basket with all the sweet-smelling
flowers and made it BEAUTIFUL for their mama.

The basket was LOVELY. But it needed something more. Trixie hopped off. Soon she returned with a plump blackberry.

Ria smiled. "Mama loves berries," she said.

So the bunnies picked berries that were juicy and ripe and perfect for bunny tummies.

PLUCK, PLUCK.
"MMM."

They filled the basket with sweetness for their mama.

At last, they were done. The BUNNIES took their

strong, beautiful, sweet basket home to their mama.

And their MAMA gave them something strong,

beautiful, and sweet right back: a big hug.

The bunnies SNUGGLED in close. "We love you, Mama," they said.

"And I love you, my bunnies," their mama replied.

Thumper
Finds a Friend

Under the warm, bright summer sun, Thumper and his sisters played tag in the forest. One bunny chased and one bunny wriggled, one bunny ducked and one bunny GIGGLED, and one bunny dove into a bush.

Behind the bush, Thumper found someone who was trying not to be found.

"Hello!" Thumper said. "Want to play tag?" But the HEDGEHOG didn't answer.

Thumper was puzzled. Didn't she want to be his friend? Then he had an idea. He would give her something SWEET. He hopped to a berry patch and picked some treats.

Thumper put some **BERRIES** next to the
hedgehog and waited. But she was still silent.
Thumper was stumped.

The hedgehog still hadn't said anything. Thumper
didn't know what to do. He hopped over to his father.
"Papa," he said, "why won't the HEDGEHOG be my
friend? I've been really nice."

Papa Bunny smiled. "Not everyone makes friends right away. Give her time," he said. Thumper nodded, and he and his sisters SCAMPERED and chased.

The bunnies jumped and joked. Thumper called out, "Do you want to be FRIENDS?" But still no hedgehog.

But when Thumper went to look behind the bush, the hedgehog was gone! GONE?

Then Thumper heard someone say in a small voice, "HELLO. May I play?"

That afternoon, five little BUNNIES and one little

hedgehog played tag in the forest.

The hedgehog chased while one bunny wriggled, and one bunny slid, and one bunny giggled, and one bunny hid, and one bunny SMILED because he made a new friend.

The crescent moon hung low, and the stars twinkled in the night sky.

All the bunnies had gone home—except Thumper. He wasn't SLEEPY yet.

Thumper hopped over to the pond. He heard a
duck softly quacking. "QUACK, QUACK."

Down near the water, a mama duck was kissing her baby ducklings good night.

SLEEP TIGHT, DUCKIES.

He hopped to an open field. In the field he found a tiny mouse washing his face with a dewdrop.

GOOD NIGHT, MOUSE.

Thumper hopped deeper into the forest. Up in a tree, a chipmunk and a squirrel drifted off to sleep.

SWEET DREAMS, FURRY FRIENDS.

Then Thumper heard a sound. He listened closely.
His MAMA was calling him. It was time to go home!

When he got home, his sisters were waiting.

"THUMPER!" they cried. "Where have you been?

We missed you!"

The bunnies SNUGGLED up together. Papa Bunny began to tell them a story.

Soon enough, all the little bunnies had fallen fast asleep—except Thumper.

Papa and Mama KISSED him. And before long, he was fast asleep, too. "Good night, Thumper," they whispered.